P9-DGI-889

♡ Eva in the Band ♡

Read more OWL DIARIES books!

OWL DIARIES

♥ Eva in the Band ♥

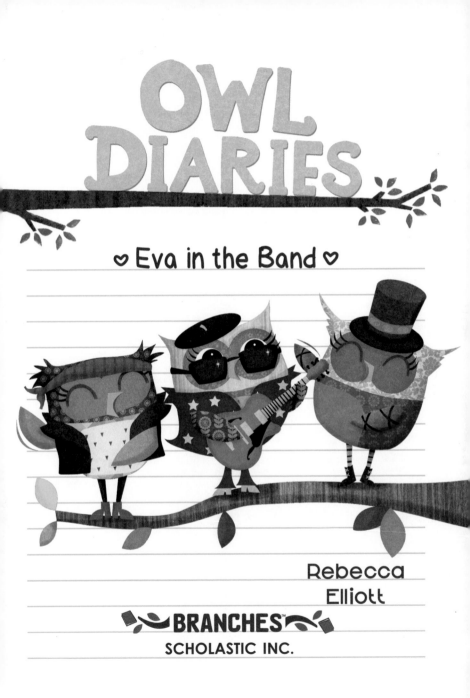

Rebecca
Elliott

BRANCHES

SCHOLASTIC INC.

For everyone I've ever been in a band with.
You guys rock. —R.E.

Special thanks to Ed Myer for
his contributions to this book.

If you purchased this book without a cover, you should be
aware that this book is stolen property. It was reported as
"unsold and destroyed" to the publisher, and neither the author nor the
publisher has received any payment for this "stripped book."

Copyright © 2022 by Rebecca Elliott

All rights reserved. Published by Scholastic Inc., *Publishers
since 1920.* SCHOLASTIC, BRANCHES, and associated logos are
trademarks and/or registered trademarks of Scholastic Inc.

The publisher does not have any control over and does not assume any
responsibility for author or third-party websites or their content.

No part of this publication may be reproduced, stored in a retrieval system, or transmitted
in any form or by any means, electronic, mechanical, photocopying, recording, or otherwise,
without written permission of the publisher. For information regarding permission, write to
Scholastic Inc., Attention: Permissions Department, 557 Broadway, New York, NY 10012.

This book is a work of fiction. Names, characters, places, and incidents are either the
product of the author's imagination or are used fictitiously, and any resemblance to actual
persons, living or dead, business establishments, events, or locales is entirely coincidental.

Library of Congress Cataloging-in-Publication Data
Names: Elliott, Rebecca, author, illustrator. | Elliott, Rebecca. Owl diaries ; 17.
Title: Eva in the band / Rebecca Elliott.
Description: First edition. | New York : Branches/Scholastic, Inc., 2022. |
Series: Owl diaries ; 17 | Audience: Ages 5–7. | Audience: Grades K–2. |
Summary: When a band drops out of Battle of the Bands Eva and her
friends decide to form a band of their own, and when a secret singer joins the
chorus it really sounds good, but she flies away before anyone can identify her.
Identifiers: LCCN 2021048798 (print) | ISBN 9781338745436 (paperback) |
ISBN 9781338745443 (library binding)
Subjects: LCSH: Owls—Juvenile fiction. | Bands (Music)—Juvenile fiction. |
Diaries—Juvenile fiction. | CYAC: Owls—Fiction. | Bands
(Music)—Fiction. | Friendship—Fiction. | Diaries—Fiction.
Classification: LCC PZ7.E45812 Epm 2022 (print)
| DDC 823.92 [Fic]—dc23/eng/20211012
LC record available at https://lccn.loc.gov/2021048798

10 9 8 7 6 5 4 3 2 1   22 23 24 25 26

Printed in China   62
First edition, December 2022

Edited by Katie Carella and Alli Brydon
Book design by Marissa Asuncion

♡ Table of Contents ♡

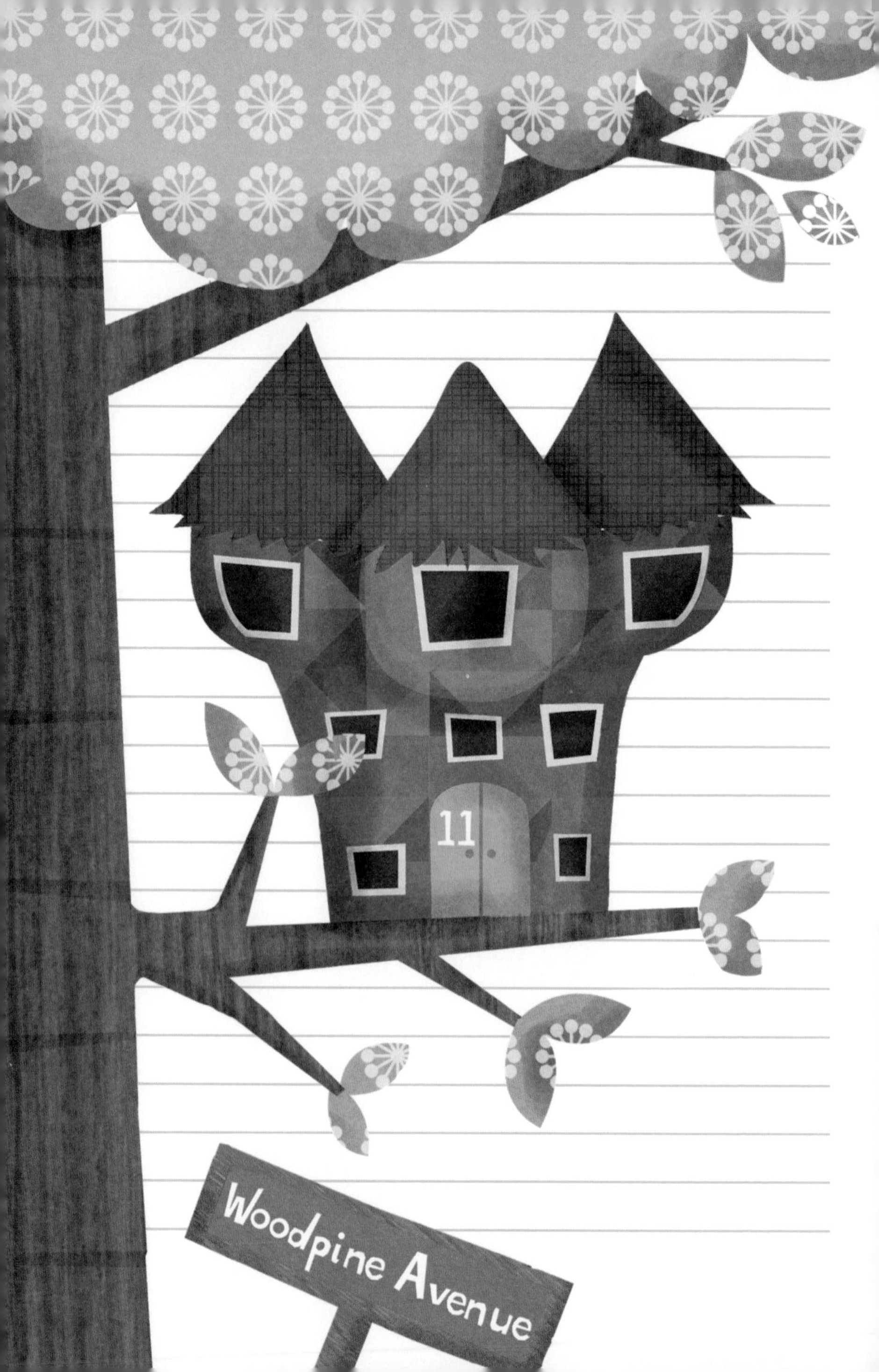
11
Woodpine Avenue

♥ HOO Wants to Dance?! ♥

Sunday

Hi Diary,

I'm so excited! My brother's band, the Hootles, is one of two bands that will be performing at the Woodlandstock Music Festival. It's next Saturday at the Old Oak Tree, and I can't wait!

I love:

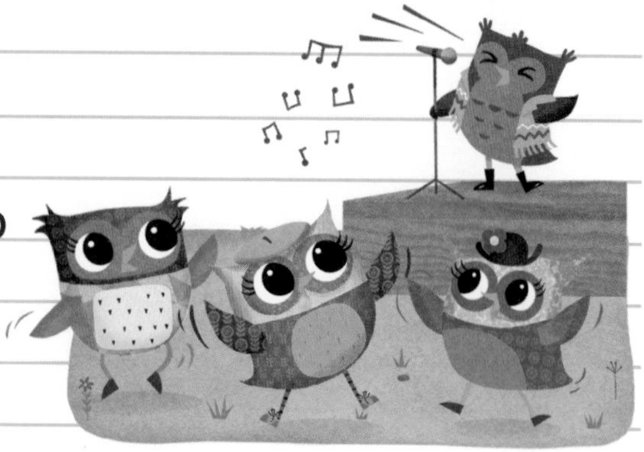

Listening to live music

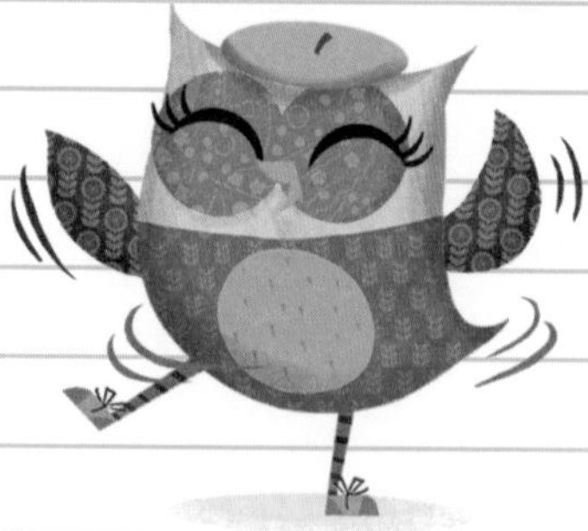

Dancing

Getting dressed up

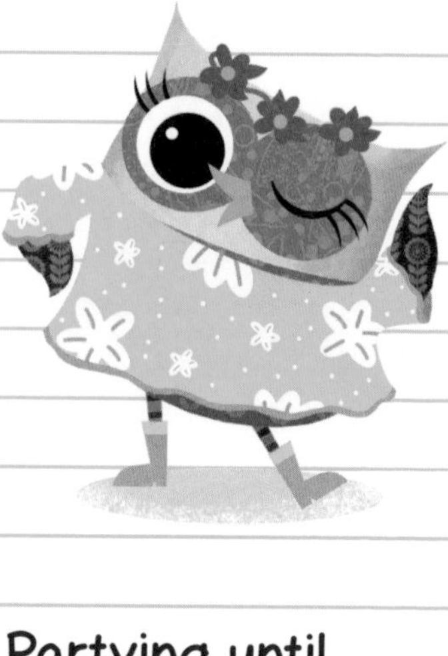

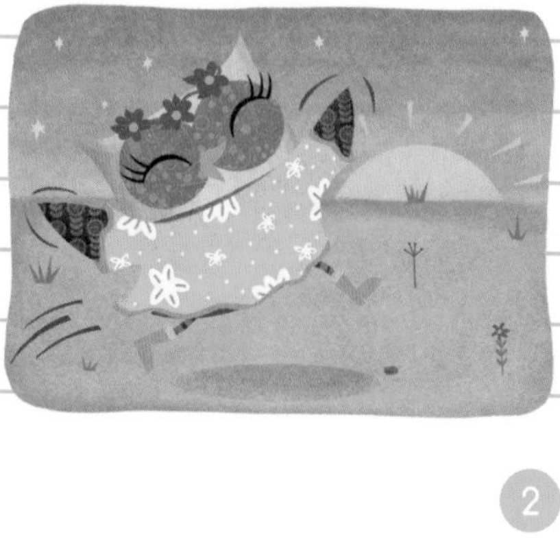

Partying until it's light

Festival food

Singing my
favorite songs

Rocking out

The word
groovy

I DO NOT love:

Humphrey's LOUD
guitar practice

My dad's terrible
singing

My mom trying to
dress cool

Having to leave
when the party's
still going

Festival toilets

Singing the wrong words

Falling down while rocking out

The word <u>stain</u>

5

This is my **FLAPTASTIC** family at a different music festival.

Dad

Mom

Me

Baby Mo

Humphrey

And these are my rockin' pets: Baxter the bat and Acorn the flying squirrel.

Being an owl is **WING-CREDIBLE**.

We can bob our heads. This is my favorite dance move!

We have super-powerful hearing.

We can fly, which means we can dance in the air!

We can hoot. We can also bark, whistle, coo, screech, and chirp!

I live at 11 Woodpine Avenue in Treetopolis. My **BFF** (Best Feathery Friend), Lucy Beakman, lives at number 9.

I have lots of friends. We go to Treetop Owlementary School. This is our class photo:

I'm trying to fall asleep, but Humphrey is practicing his guitar!

2

♡ Oh No! ♡

Monday

At breakfast, we were enjoying bug pancakes and acorn syrup.

I can't wait for the music festival!

Yeah, Woodlandstock is going to be totally <u>owlsome</u>!

Humphrey answered the **PINEPHONE**.
Then he told us something <u>terrible</u>!

I couldn't believe it!

At school, everyone was still excited about the music festival.

Then Mrs. Featherbottom looked at me.

My cheeks went red.

I could feel myself about to cry.
Thankfully, it was time for recess.

I sat alone singing one of the Hootles' songs. I felt embarrassed about almost crying in front of everyone. And I was so sad the festival was canceled.

Lucy and Hailey flew over.

Eva, it must have felt horrible telling everyone the bad news.

We were all looking forward to the music festival.

Can't they find another band?

Not in less than a week!

Now, <u>that</u> got me thinking for the rest of the night. It would be amazing to become a rock star! Maybe I could save the festival!

But what would Humphrey think?

I told Humphrey about Lucy's idea while we did the dishes after dinner.

So, what do you think? Could I save the festival?!

Um . . . thank you, Eva. It's a nice idea, but the festival needs a <u>band</u>. Not just one singer.

I really wanted to help, so — without thinking — I said . . .

I looked around the room and blurted out the first things I saw.

I crossed my **FEATHERS** hoping Humphrey would say yes.

That's a pretty cool name. And it <u>would</u> be great to have the festival.

If you let the Flying Bluebells play, I will do the dishes for a whole month!

Hmm.

Oh, Diary, I can't wait to sing at the festival! Just one problem — I need to find a band to play with!! Any ideas?

♡ Let's Band Together ♡

Tuesday

I told Lucy and Hailey about the Flying Bluebells the moment I got to school.

Will you two be in my band?

Oh, wow! Really? Thanks, Eva!

I've always wanted to be in a band.

Then welcome to the Flying Bluebells!

Mrs. Featherbottom flew over.

She **HOOTED** to the class.

Everyone — stop what you're doing! We have a new class project. We're forming a band!

We're called the Flying Bluebells!

And we'll perform at the Woodlandstock Music Festival.

Remember, class, this festival will raise money for our school library. More books for all!

The whole class was excited about the band.

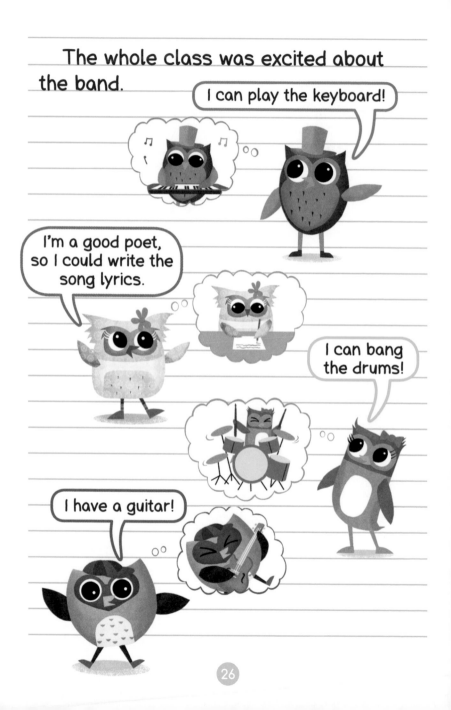

I can play the keyboard!

I'm a good poet, so I could write the song lyrics.

I can bang the drums!

I have a guitar!

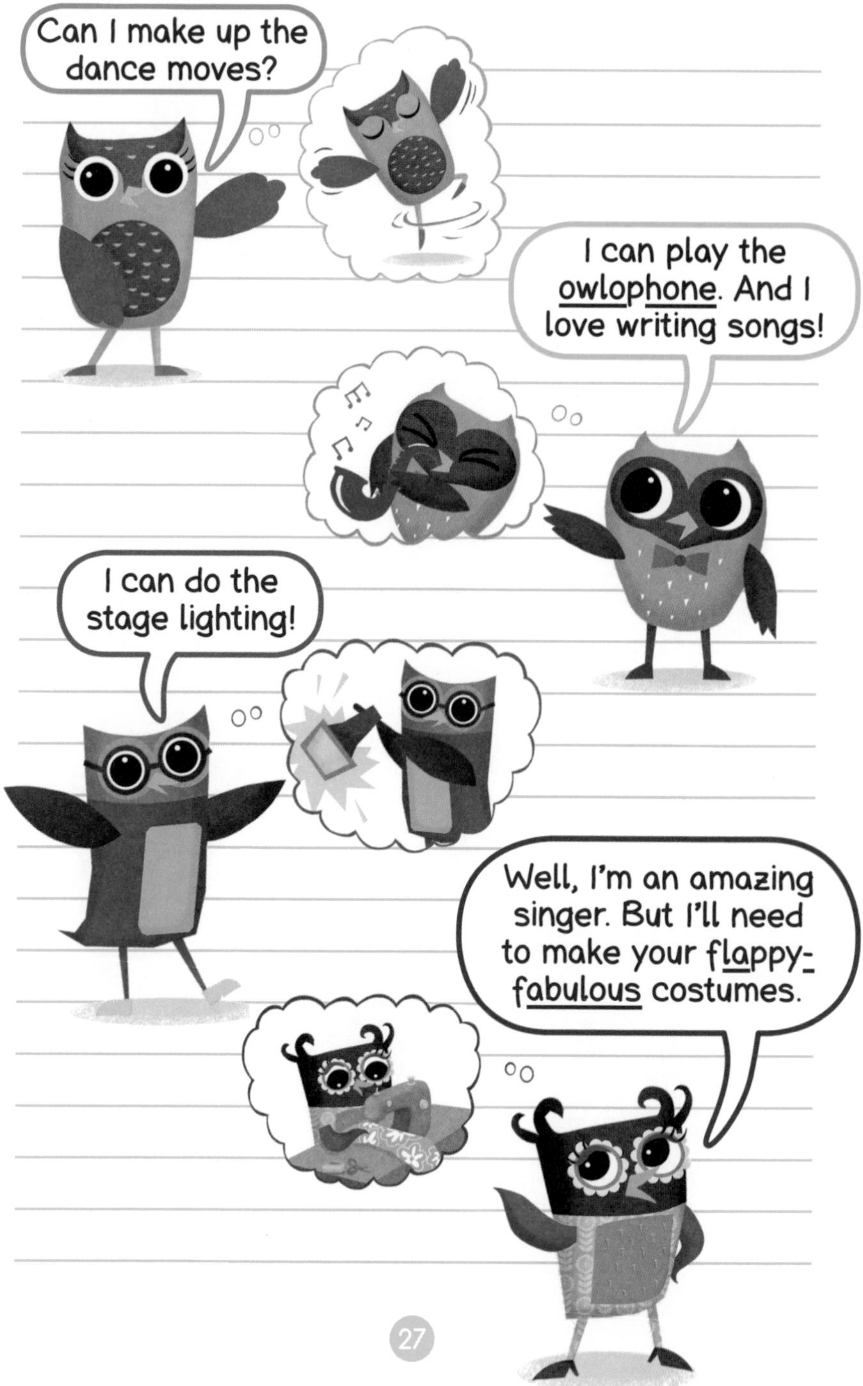
Can I make up the dance moves?
I can play the owlophone. And I love writing songs!
I can do the stage lighting!
Well, I'm an amazing singer. But I'll need to make your flappy-fabulous costumes.

Zara hung back, looking a bit shy.

It turns out our whole class was super talented!

After school, Lucy, Hailey, and I practiced a new song Kiera wrote tonight called "Owl around the World." Kiera and Jacob sat next to us, writing another **FLAPTASTIC** song called "The Big Bird Boogie-Boo."

Zac flew past.

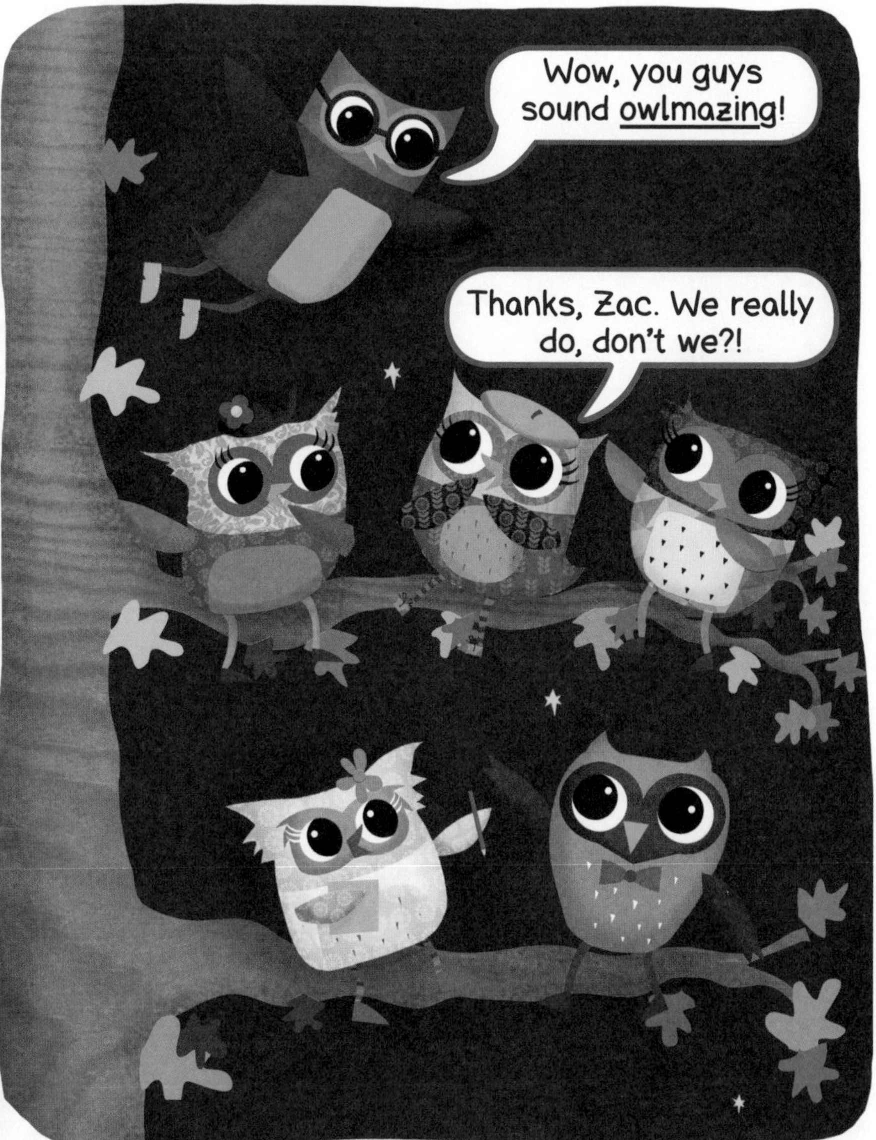
Wow, you guys sound owlmazing!
Thanks, Zac. We really do, don't we?!

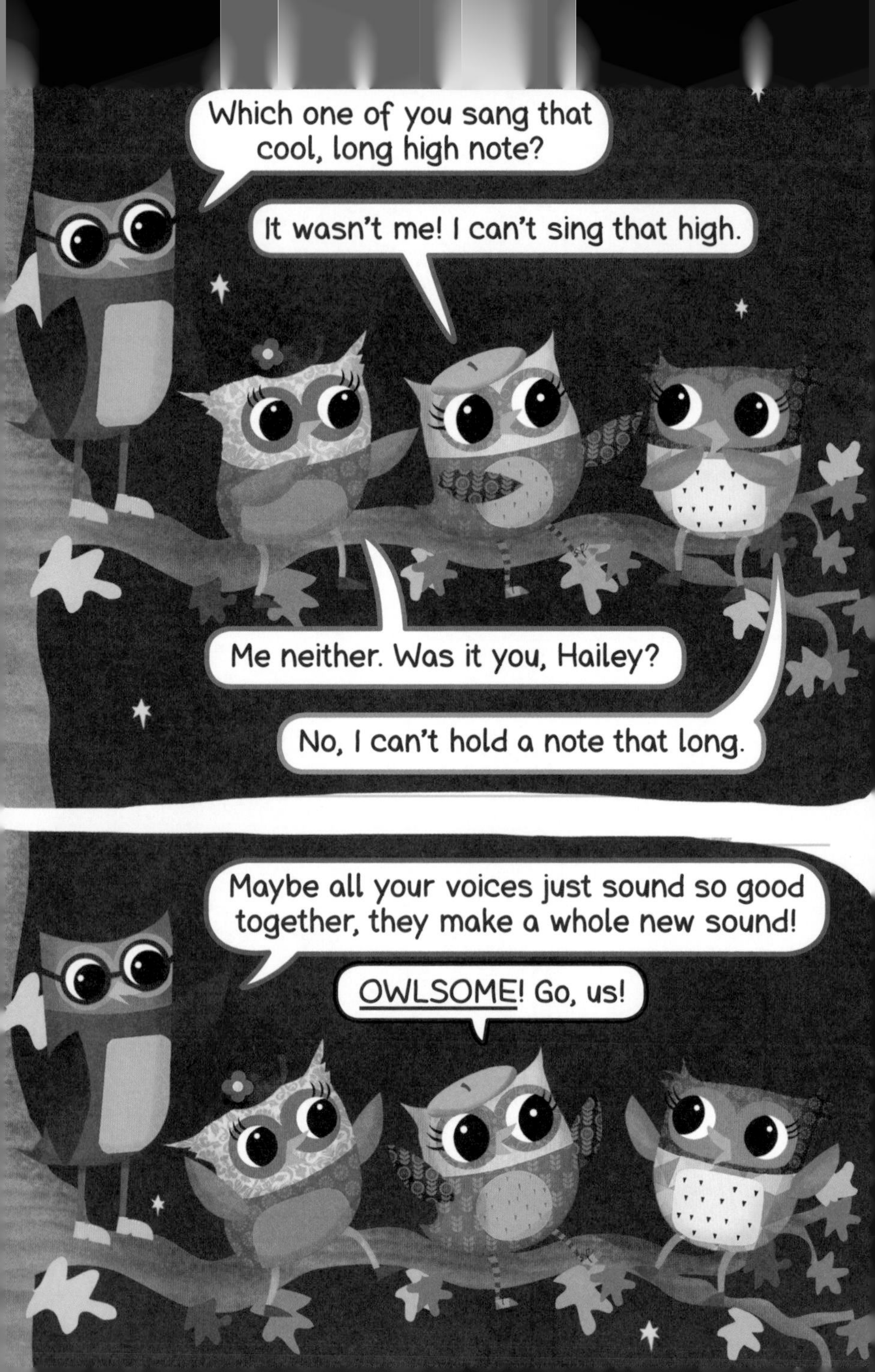
Which one of you sang that cool, long high note?
It wasn't me! I can't sing that high.
Me neither. Was it you, Hailey?
No, I can't hold a note that long.
Maybe all your voices just sound so good together, they make a whole new sound!
OWLSOME! Go, us!

After practice, we all went home. I had so much fun singing that I was still singing at bedtime!

♡ Shaking Our Tail Feathers ♡

Wednesday

At school, Lucy, Hailey, Carlos, George, Jacob, Macy, and I put on the costumes that Sue and Zara had made.

Then Lilly taught us a dance move where we all shake our tail feathers to the music. It was so funny!

We were all shaking so hard to the music that . . .

. . . our costumes ripped!

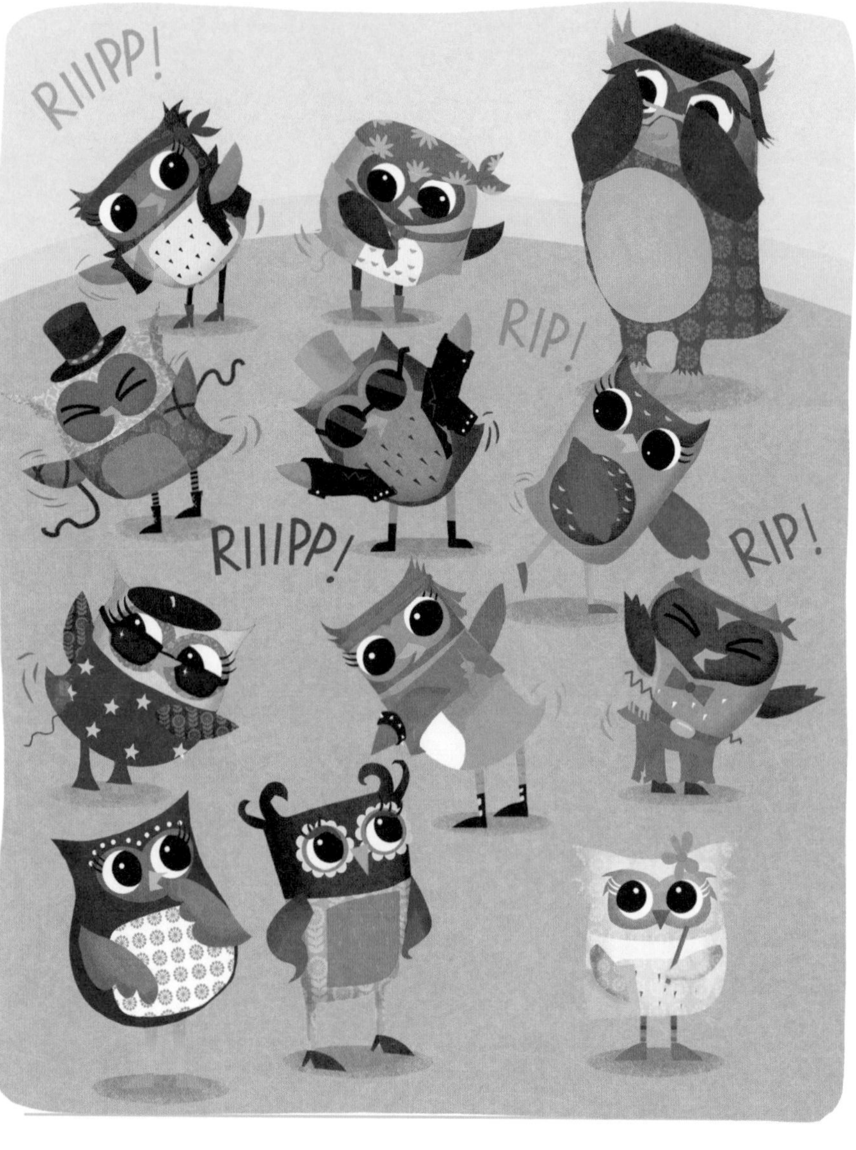
RIIIPP!
RIP!
RIIIPP!
RIP!

We kept practicing the songs.
But somehow our singing didn't sound
as good as it had sounded the day before.

After school, we flew around the forest. We left a flyer on every door so everyone would know about the music festival.

Here's the flyer:

WOODLANDSTOCK MUSIC FESTIVAL

Rock out to raise money for the school library!

★ Featuring:

THE HOOTLES and THE FLYING BLUEBELLS

★ Where: The Old Oak Tree

★ When: Saturday at 3:00 a.m.

★ Come hungry – there will be food stalls!

COTTON CANDY

HOT DOGS

On our way home, we saw Zara sitting alone.

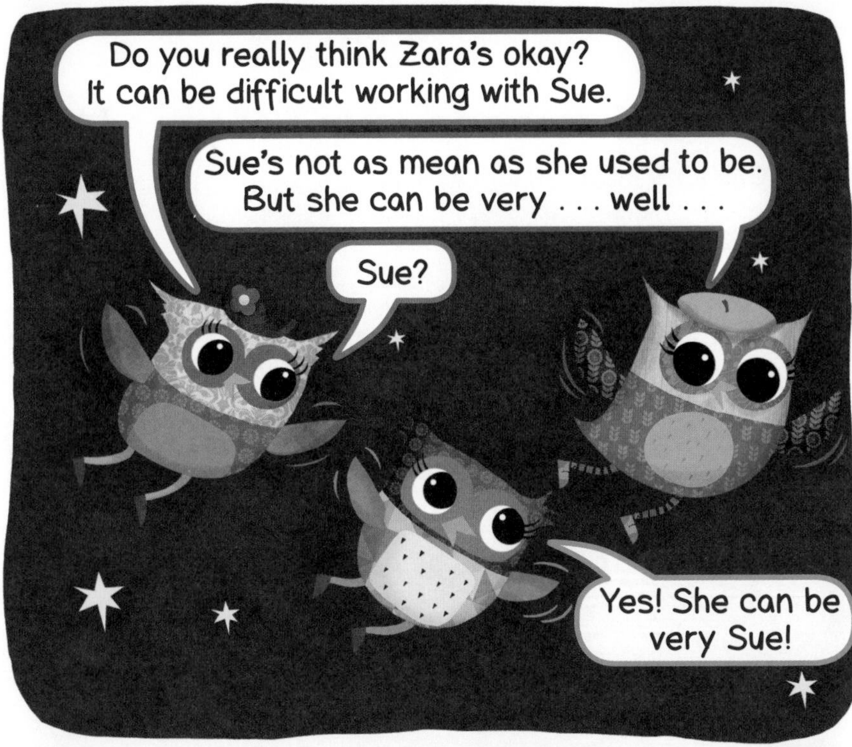
Do you really think Zara's okay? It can be difficult working with Sue.
Sue's not as mean as she used to be. But she can be very . . . well . . .
Sue?
Yes! She can be very Sue!

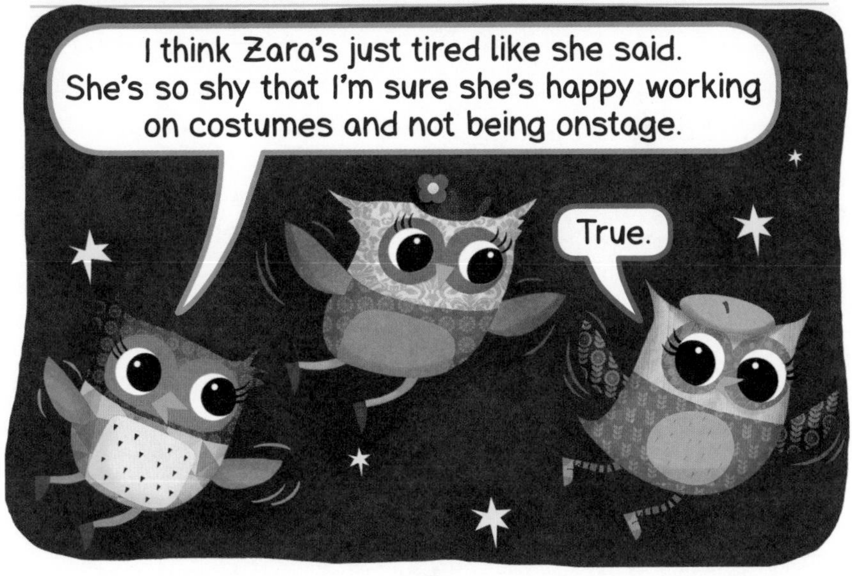
I think Zara's just tired like she said. She's so shy that I'm sure she's happy working on costumes and not being onstage.
True.

Back at my house, Lucy, Hailey, and I practiced singing again.

Lucy and Hailey tried to sing the high note, too. But all that came out was:

We didn't know that anyone heard us, but . . .

Humphrey had been listening the whole time. He burst into my room!

Owl. My. Goodness. You three sound AWFUL! We'll have to cancel the festival after all!

No, Humphrey – wait!

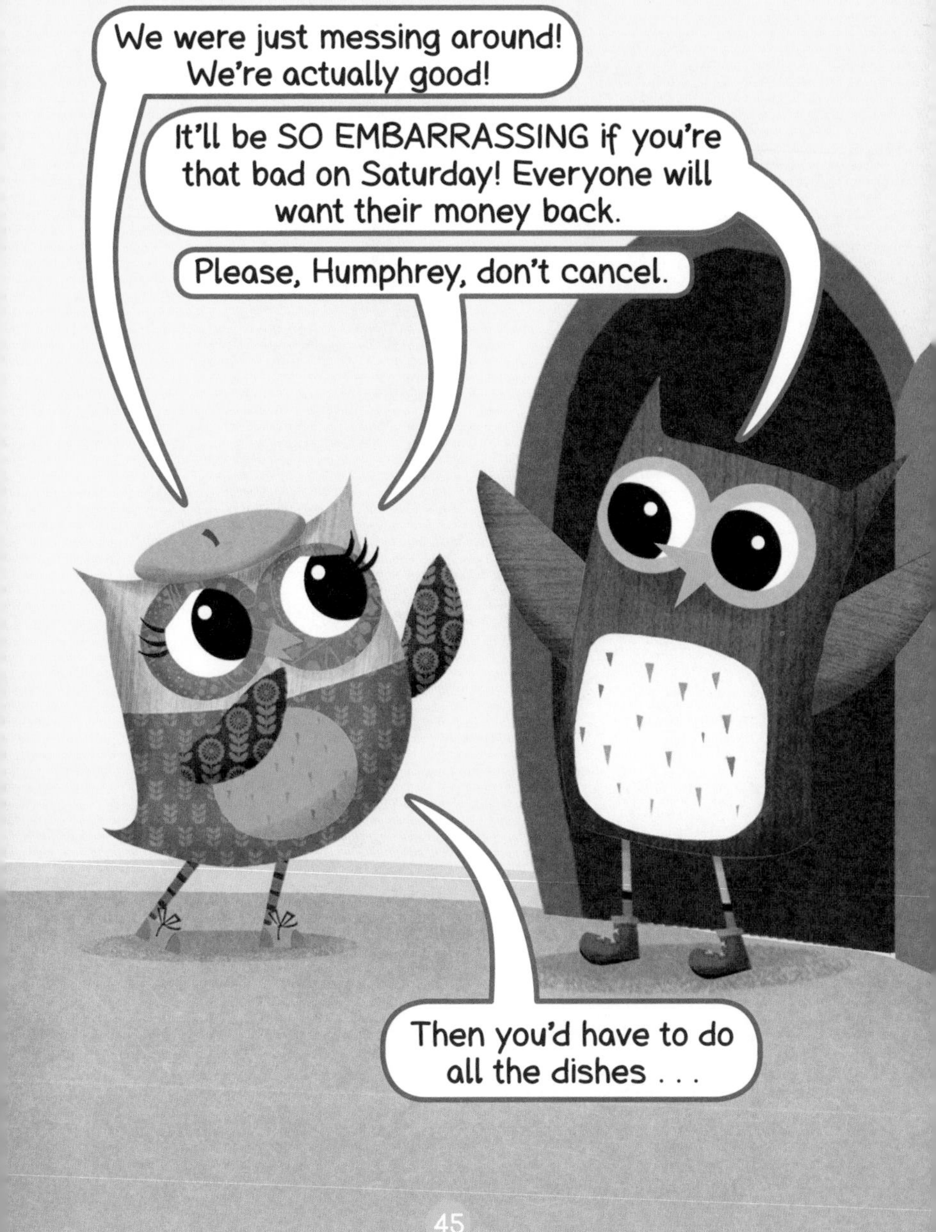
We were just messing around! We're actually good!
It'll be SO EMBARRASSING if you're that bad on Saturday! Everyone will want their money back.
Please, Humphrey, don't cancel.
Then you'd have to do all the dishes . . .

Oh dear, Diary! Now our band <u>really</u> has to be great, or the festival will get canceled AGAIN . . . after all our hard work! Better get some sleep so I can practice real hard tomorrow. Night night!

♡The Secret Singer ♡

Thursday

I told everyone about how the Hootles wanted us to perform for them. We have to sound good by the end of the night or the festival will be canceled.

You can do this, Flying Bluebells!

Humphrey's band met us outside after school. It was time for us to show our stuff. And — oh, Diary — it did NOT go well! We forgot some of the words and had to **HOOT** instead!

Let's all do the Big Bird Boogie-Boo! You can even sing along, too! Everybody copy our moves! Um—hoot hoot hoot hoot hoot hoot!

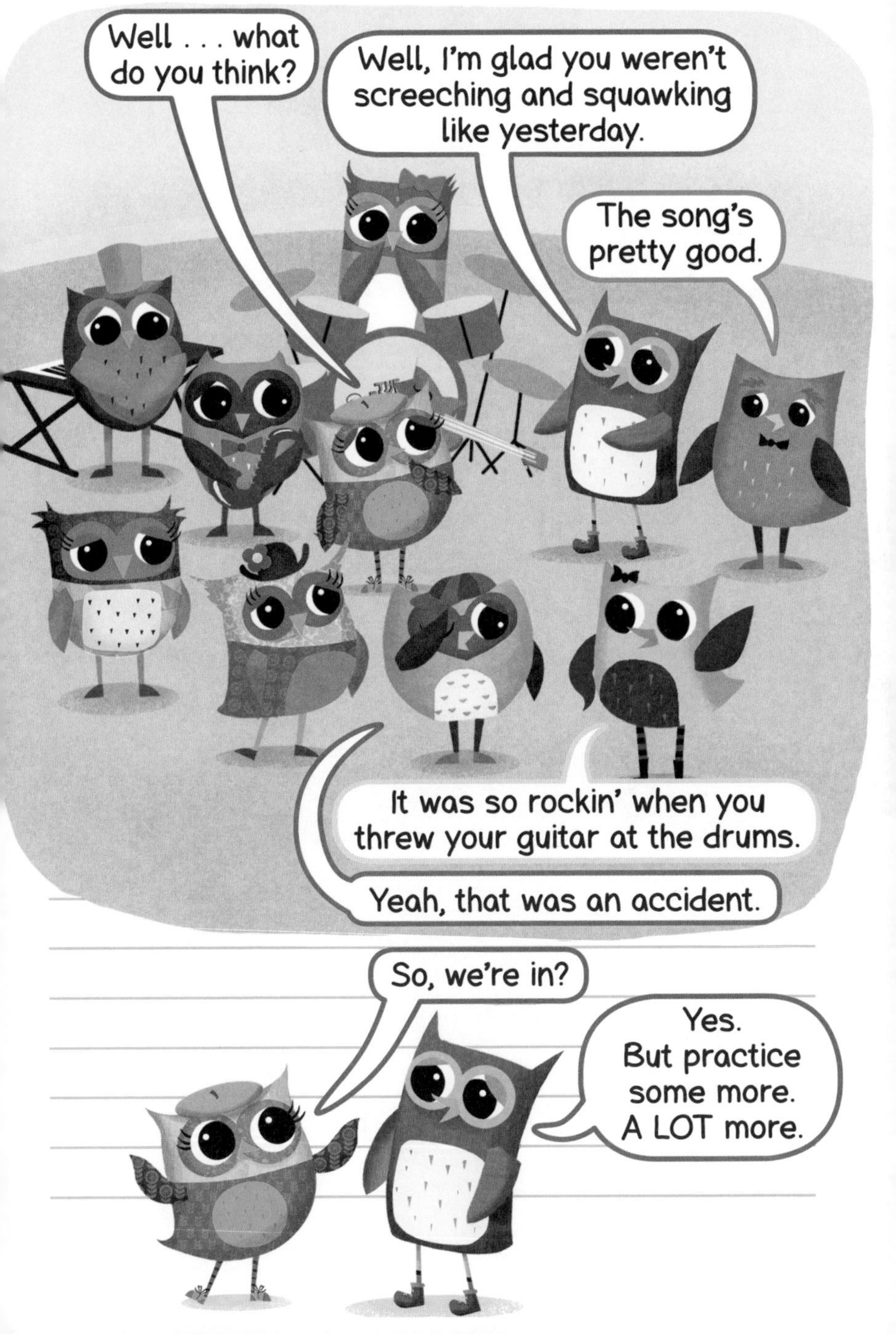
Well . . . what do you think?
Well, I'm glad you weren't screeching and squawking like yesterday.
The song's pretty good.
It was so rockin' when you threw your guitar at the drums.
Yeah, that was an accident.
So, we're in?
Yes. But practice some more. A LOT more.

We felt happy that the festival was still on, but disappointed we had more work to do. Lucy, Hailey, and I practiced the song on our way home. Suddenly, we sounded **OWLMAZING** again!

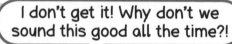

I don't get it! Why don't we sound this good all the time?!

Then Lucy had an idea. She whispered to us.

Someone is singing with us! And I know how to find out who it is! Start singing again!

We sang again. Then Lucy put up her wing, and we all stopped. But the singing didn't stop! A **HOOTIFUL** voice sang for a bit longer.

Come out, whoever you are! You have an amazing voice. Don't be shy!

But the secret singer did not come out.

Back at my house, we ate **BEETLE BROWNIES** and talked about our discovery.

So the reason we sounded good before was because someone ELSE was singing with us.

That voice is <u>wing-credible</u>! The truth is, we don't sound very good without it.

Who could it be?

It must be someone from our class who knows the songs.

We came up with a
plan to find the secret
singer. I'll tell you more
tomorrow, Diary!

♡ OWL Together Now ♡

Friday

At school, we put our plan into action.

Just to help us practice, we thought it would be cool if we all sang part of "Owl around the World" together.

SCREECH

54

We wrote out some of the words so everyone could sing along. Zara held them up while we all sang. Lucy, Hailey, and I tried to listen for the secret singer.

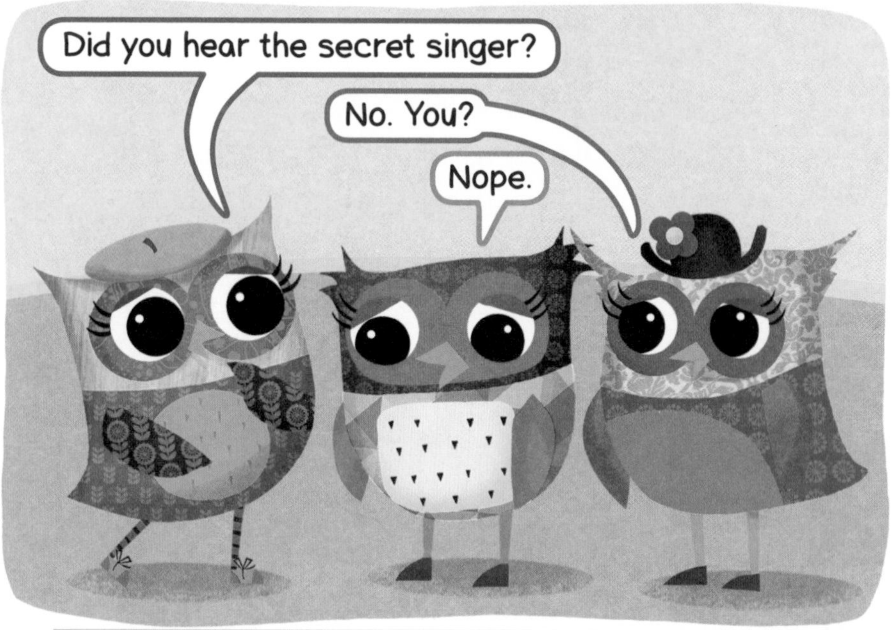
Did you hear the secret singer?
No. You?
Nope.

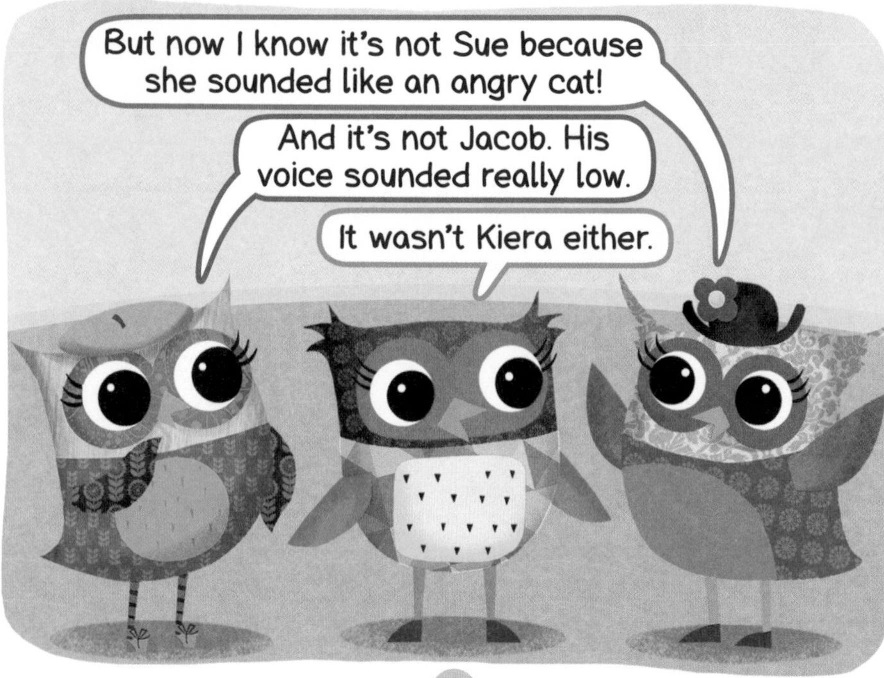
But now I know it's not Sue because she sounded like an angry cat!
And it's not Jacob. His voice sounded really low.
It wasn't Kiera either.

Hailey, Lucy, and I felt disappointed. But all we can do is perform our best. Hopefully we don't sound too bad without those lovely high notes in our songs.

Next, we practiced our dance moves.
At least we'll <u>look</u> groovy onstage!

I've drawn out all the moves! When I
hold a card up, just move how it says.

We started getting the moves right
and having lots of fun, too!

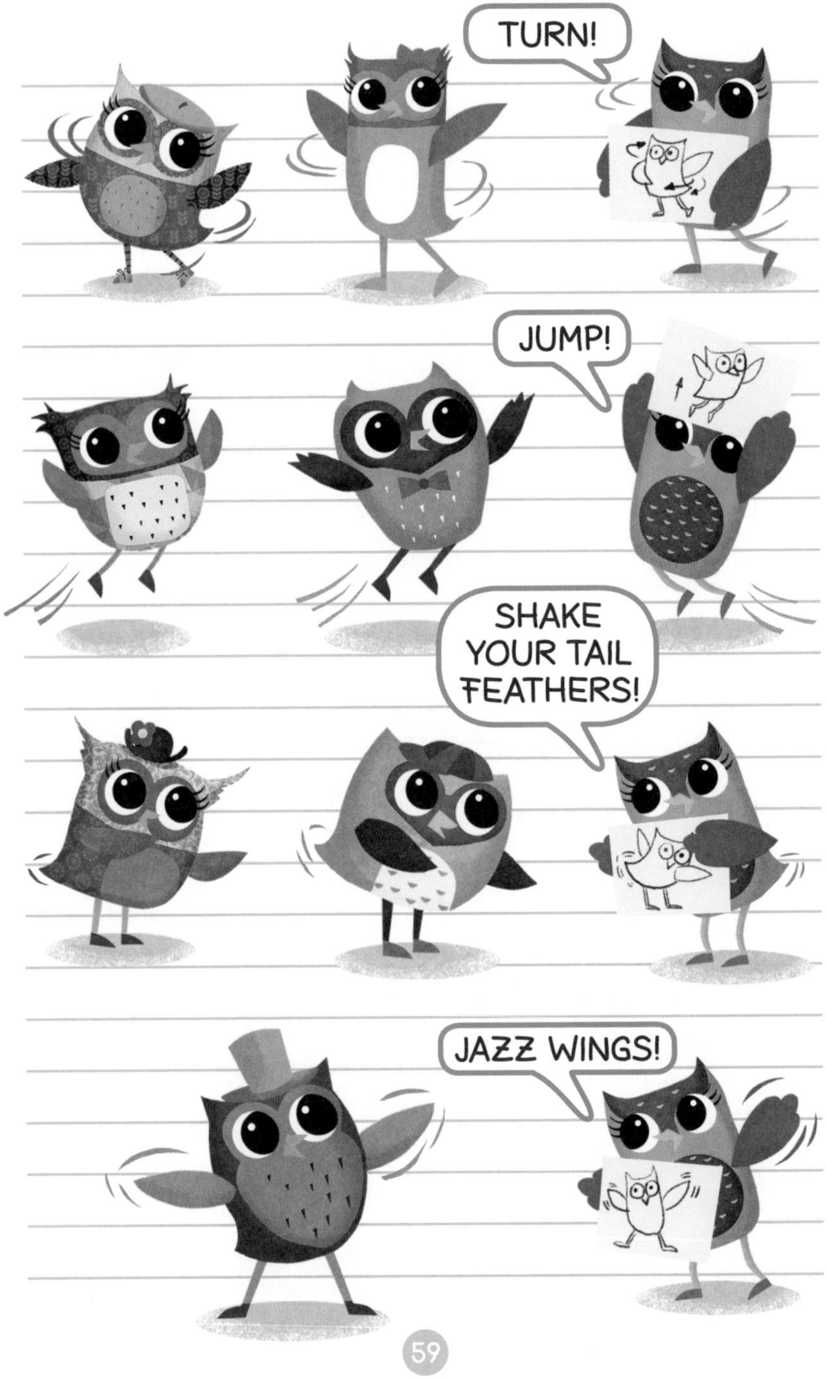
TURN!
JUMP!
SHAKE YOUR TAIL FEATHERS!
JAZZ WINGS!

Suddenly, I had a thought while watching Lilly hold up the cards.

Thankfully, it was time for recess, so I could tell Hailey and Lucy what I was thinking. I dragged them to a quiet corner.

When we all sang together, <u>Zara</u> held up the word cards!

So?

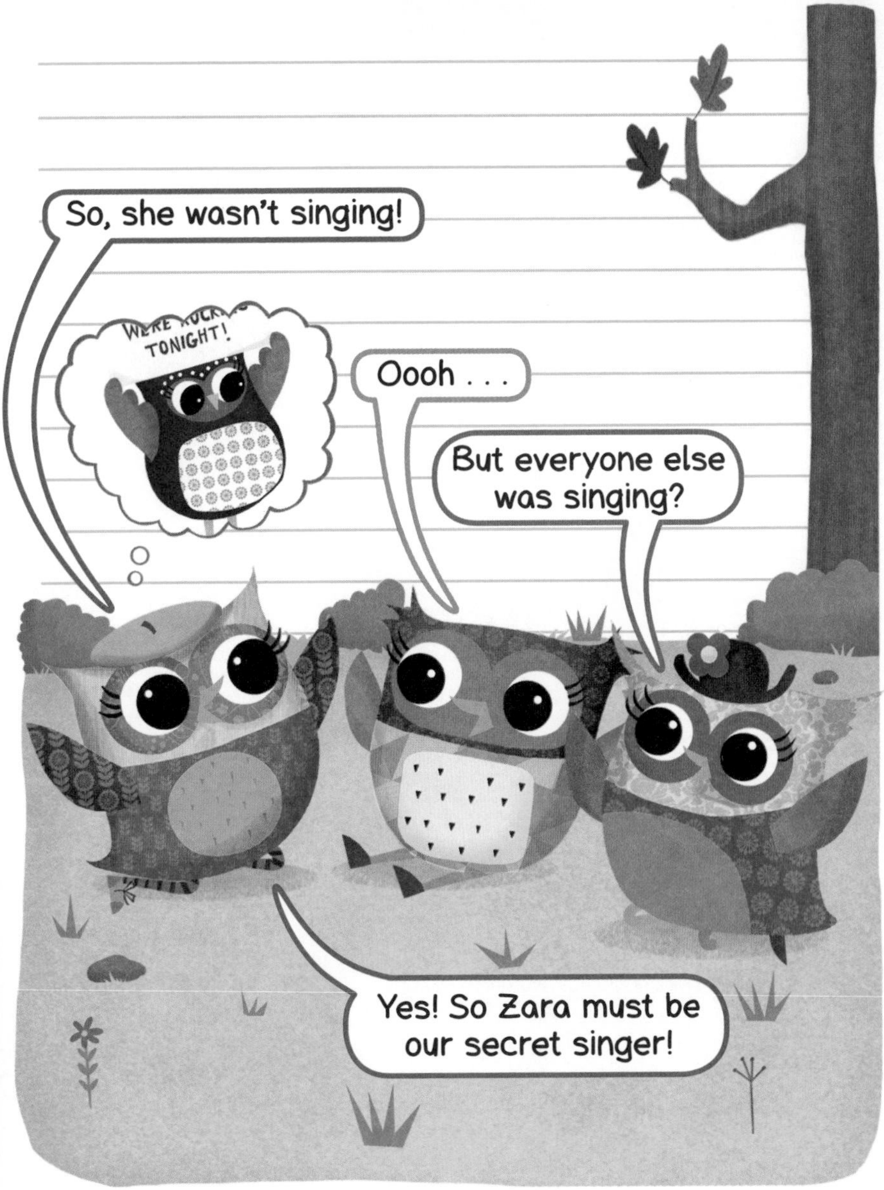
So, she wasn't singing!
TONIGHT!
Oooh . . .
But everyone else was singing?
Yes! So Zara must be our secret singer!

We flew over to Zara.

Zara, were you secretly singing along with us in the trees?
Oh! Yes. Sorry about that.
Don't be sorry! You have the most wing-credible voice!

I felt bad for Zara. She had such an
OWLMAZING voice. But her shyness was
stopping her from showing it off.

Then Sue swooped down.

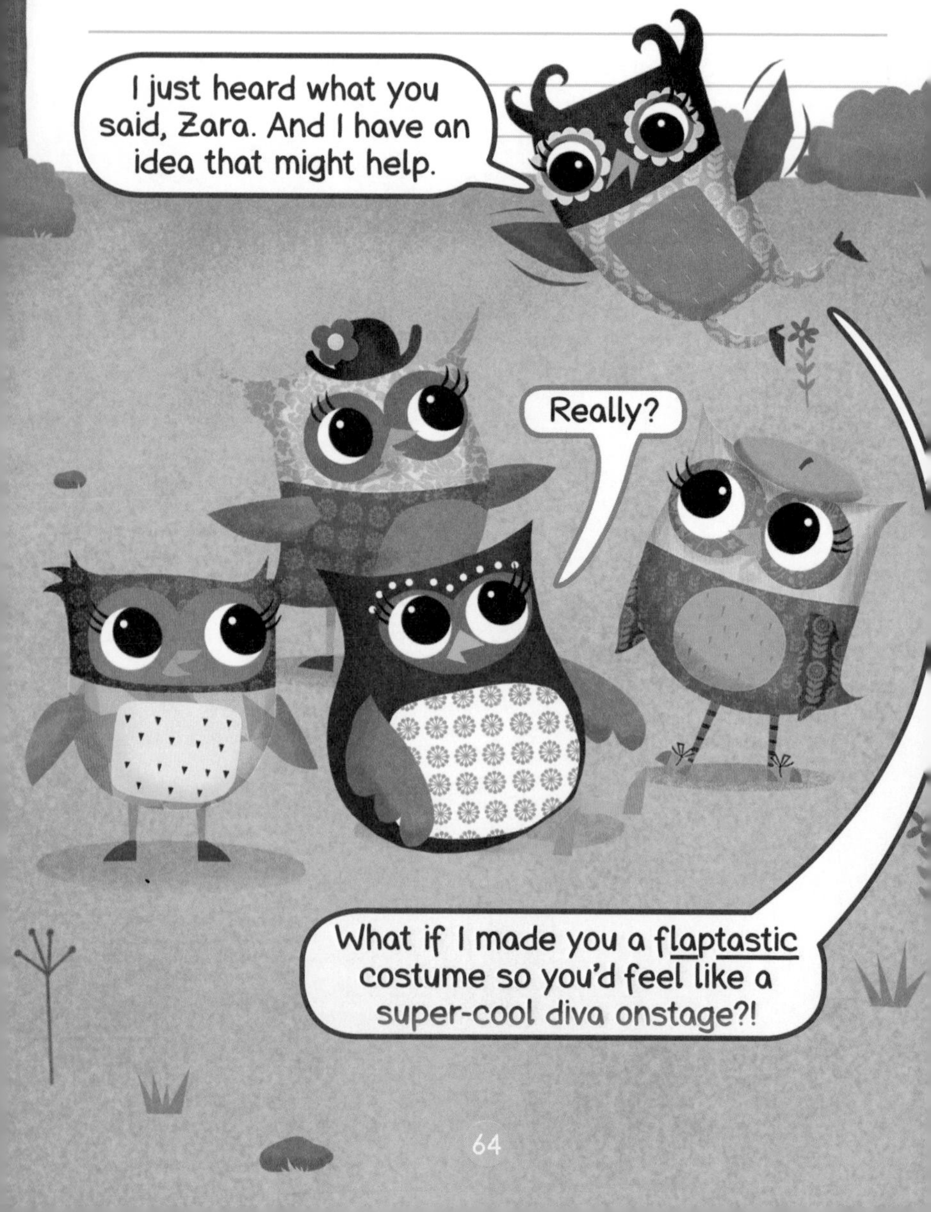

I just heard what you said, Zara. And I have an idea that might help.
Really?
What if I made you a flaptastic costume so you'd feel like a super-cool diva onstage?!

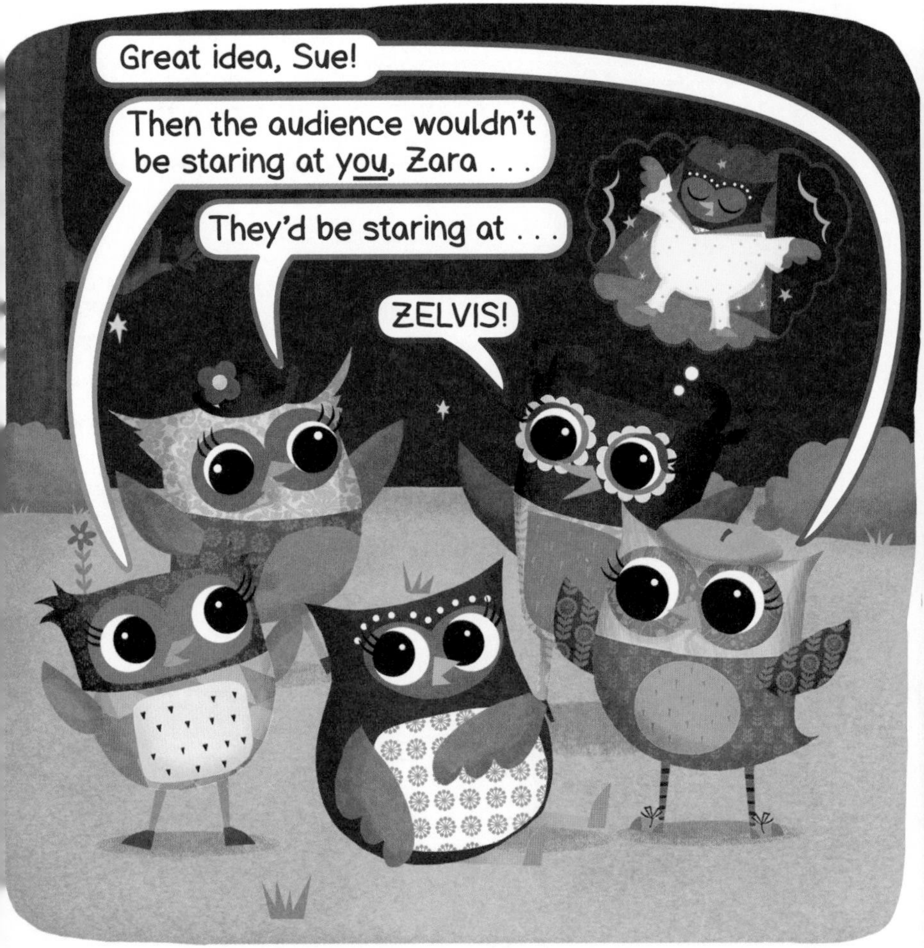
Great idea, Sue!
Then the audience wouldn't be staring at you, Zara . . .
They'd be staring at . . .
ZELVIS!

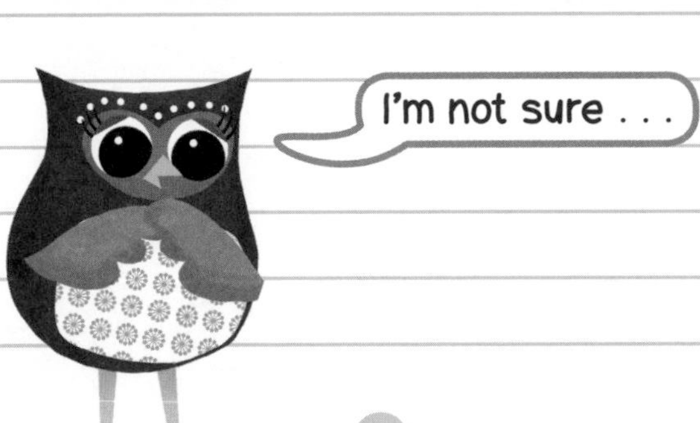
I'm not sure . . .

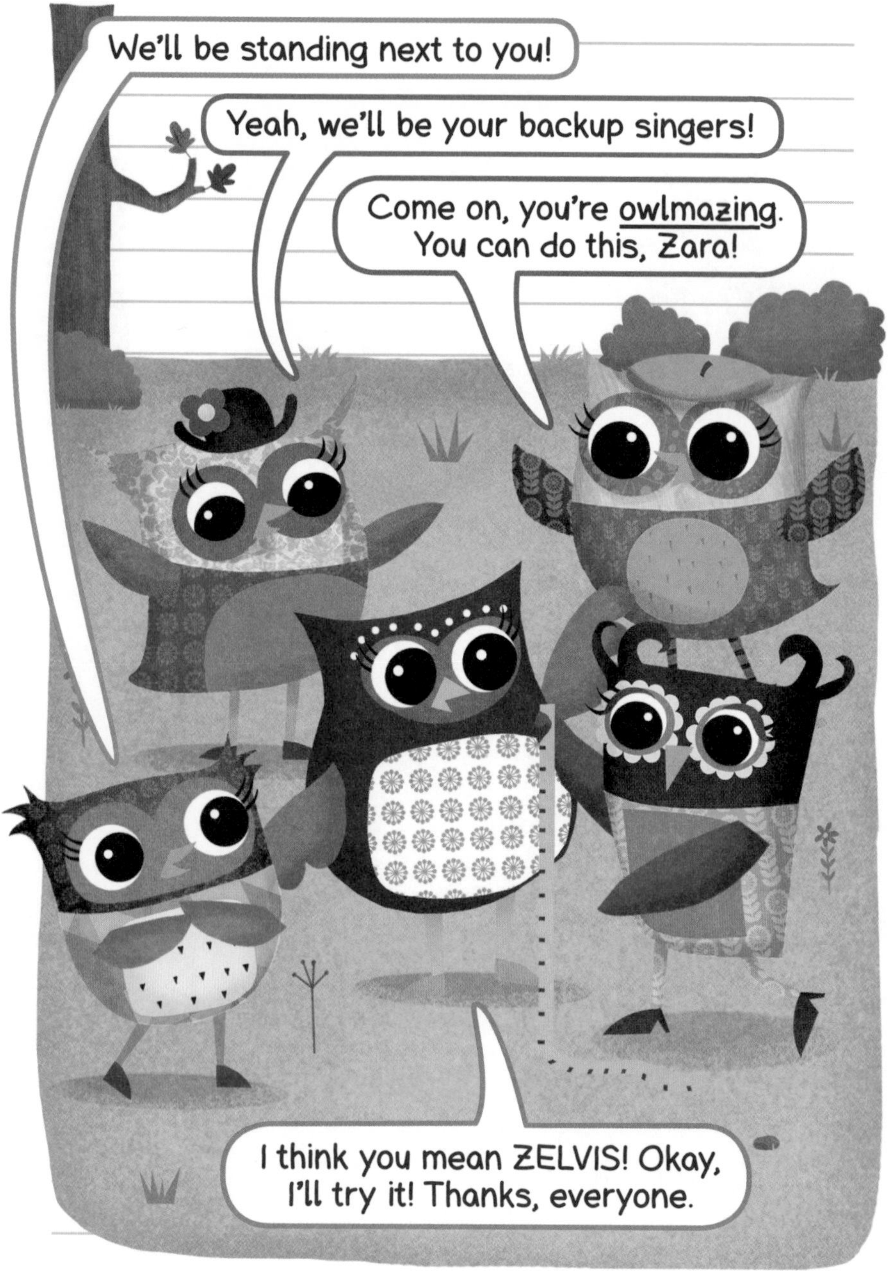
We'll be standing next to you!
Yeah, we'll be your backup singers!
Come on, you're owlmazing. You can do this, Zara!
I think you mean ZELVIS! Okay, I'll try it! Thanks, everyone.

I'm feeling excited <u>and</u> nervous about tomorrow! I just hope none of us forget what to do onstage. And I REALLY hope Zara goes through with the show. Then maybe – just maybe – we might not get booed off the stage!

♡ Let's Rock! ♡

Saturday

It was finally time for us to perform at the Woodlandstock Music Festival.

Everyone cheered as we walked out. I felt like a real rock star!

But Zara wasn't onstage yet. Had she changed her mind about singing?

Just then, Zara flew onto the stage in her **OWLSOME** costume, with a sparkly cape fluttering behind her.

We danced and sang. And when Zara hit that long, high note, the crowd roared!

The Hootles came out next.

Wow! The Flying Bluebells ROCK! Special thanks goes to my sister, Eva, for putting that band together. Eva saved this festival!

AND we've raised lots of money for our school library!

THE HOOTLES

Three cheers for Eva!

My face went red, but I was so happy!

Now that Woodlandstock is over, I can tell you, Diary — being a rock star is tiring! But I think we can do one more song . . .

See you next time, Diary!

Rebecca Elliott was a lot like Eva when she was younger: She loved making things and hanging out with her best friends. Now that Rebecca is older, not much has changed — except that her best friends now include her two sons, Benjy and Toby. She still loves making things, like stories, cakes, music, and paintings. But as much as she and Eva have in common, Rebecca cannot fly or turn her head all the way around. No matter how hard she tries.

Rebecca is the author of several picture books, the young adult novel PRETTY FUNNY FOR A GIRL, and the bestselling UNICORN DIARIES and OWL DIARIES early chapter book series.

OWL DIARIES

How much do you know about Eva in the Band?

How does Eva come up with her band name, the Flying Bluebells?

Why does Humphrey agree to let Eva's band perform at the festival? Reread Chapter 2.

Who is the secret singer? How do Eva, Lucy, and Hailey figure out who it is?

At first, Zara feels too shy to go onstage. How does Sue convince Zara to sing in the band?

How does each of my classmates get involved with the Flying Bluebells? Draw them all helping out and add labels to explain what they're doing.